Level 1 is i
some initial r
or subjects ar
number of fre

Special features:

mouse

elephant

water

hunter

forest

net

6

7

Opening pages
introduce key
story words

Large,
clear type

One day, some elephants
went to the water.

The mice saw the
elephants. They
were afraid.

Careful match
between text
and pictures

10

11

Educational Consultant: Geraldine Taylor
Book Banding Consultant: Kate Ruttle

LADYBIRD BOOKS

UK | USA | Canada | Ireland | Australia
India | New Zealand | South Africa

Ladybird Books is part of the Penguin Random House group of companies
whose addresses can be found at global.penguinrandomhouse.com.

www.penguin.co.uk www.puffin.co.uk www.ladybird.co.uk

Penguin
Random House
UK

First published 2019
001

Copyright © Ladybird Books Ltd, 2019

Printed in China

A CIP catalogue record for this book is available from the British Library

ISBN: 978-0-241-36144-3

All correspondence to
Ladybird Books
Penguin Random House Children's Books
80 Strand, London WC2R 0RL

The Mice and the Elephants

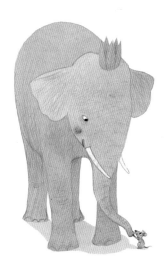

Retold by Monica Hughes

Illustrated by Mar Ferrero

mouse

elephant

forest

water

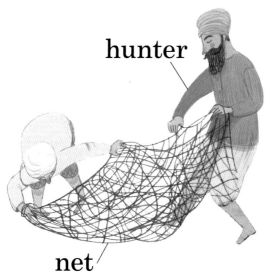

hunter

net

7

The mice had always
lived by the water.

And the elephants had always lived in the forest.

One day, some elephants went to the water.

The mice saw the elephants. They were afraid.

But the Mouse King
was not afraid.

He went to the
Elephant King.

12

"The mice are afraid of the elephants," he said.

"Tell the mice not to
be afraid," said the
Elephant King.
"We will go to the
water another way."

14

The elephants went to
the water another way.

"The mice will always help the elephants," said the Mouse King.

Some hunters lived by the forest. The hunters had nets.

One day, they were out in the forest. They saw the elephants.

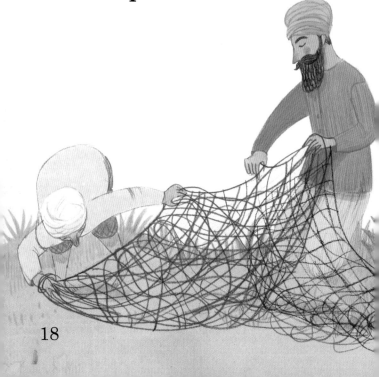

Some of the elephants
were in the hunters' nets!

The elephants were
afraid of the hunters.

But the Elephant King
was not afraid.

"Go and tell the
Mouse King," he said.
"The mice will help us."

"Some elephants are in the hunters' nets!" said the elephant.

And the mice went into the forest to help the elephants.

The mice had good
teeth. Their teeth went
into the nets.

The elephants were out!

"We will always help the elephants," said the Mouse King. "And the elephants will always help us."

29

How much do you remember about
The Mice and the Elephants?
Answer these questions and find out!

- What were the mice
  afraid of?

- What were the elephants
  afraid of?

- How did the mice help
  the elephants?